Library of Congress Cataloging in Publication Data

Vincent, Gabrielle.   Ernest and Célestine's picnic.
Translation of: Ernest et Célestine vont pique-niquer.
Summary: Rain does not stop Ernest
and Celestine from picnicking.
[1. Picnicking—Fiction.   2. Bears—Fiction.
3. Mice—Fiction]   I. Title.
PZ7.V744Es   [E]   82-2909
ISBN 0-688-01250-7   AACR2
ISBN 0-688--01252-3 (lib. bdg.)

GABRIELLE VINCENT

Ernest and Celestine's Picnic

GREENWILLOW BOOKS
NEW YORK

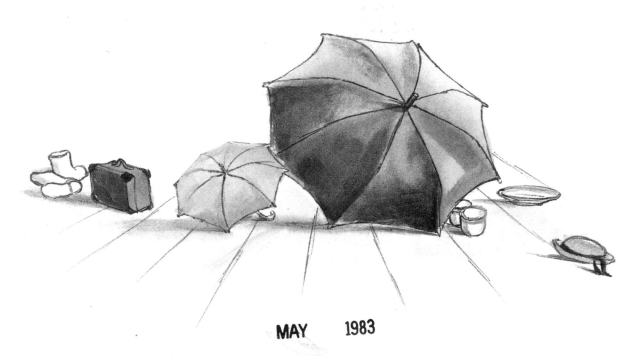

"There, Celestine. Honey sandwiches for me and cheese sandwiches for you. Everything is ready for our picnic tomorrow."

8303238

"It's going to be the best picnic ever."

"I'll put everything together, Ernest."

"Hurray! We're going on a picnic! I'll see you
when we get home, Gideon. Here I come, Ernest!"

"But, Celestine, we can't go. It's pouring."

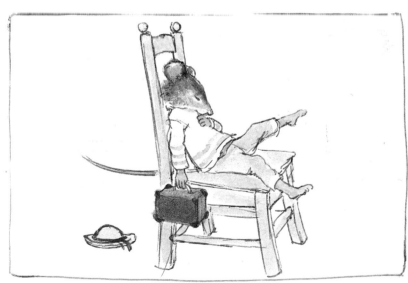

"Please, Celestine, be sensible."

"All right, Celestine, I have an idea. Shall we pretend the sun is shining?"
"Oh, what a beautiful morning!"

"Hats are good for sun and rain, aren't they, Ernest?"

"Really, Ernest, can't you see it's raining?"

"Don't be silly. It's a lovely day."

"Here's a good place, Ernest."

"A perfect picnic spot!"

"And a perfect picnic, Ernest."

"Listen, Celestine, someone's coming."

"What are you doing here? This is private property."

"We didn't mean to trespass. Do you want us to leave?"
"Well, it's all right just this once, I suppose."

"Wait a minute. Won't you have a cup of tea with us?"

"And so, we decided to pretend the sun was shining...."

"I visited you in your tent, now you must come to my house with me."

"And next week, if it's sunny, we'll all have a picnic outside together!"